The HUNDREDth
ANNIVERSARY
CELEBRATION

The HUNDREDth ANNIVERSARY CELEBRATION

EDITED BY PETER GLASSMAN

BOOKS OF WONDER

HARPERCOLLINSPUBLISHERS

Oz: The Hundredth Anniversary Celebration
Introduction copyright © 2000 by Peter Glassman
Each individual contribution copyright © 2000 by the individual contributor

Library of Congress Cataloging-in-Publication Data
Oz: the hundredth anniversary celebration / edited by Peter Glassman.— 1st ed.
    p.   cm. — (Books of wonder)
    Summary: Various writers and artists express the influence that the book
"The Wizard of Oz" had on them.
    ISBN 0-688-15915-X
    1. Baum, L. Frank (Lyman Frank), 1856–1919. Wizard of Oz—Juvenile
literature.   2. Children's stories, American—History and criticism—Juvenile
literature.   3. Fantasy fiction, American—History and criticism—
Juvenile literature.   4. Oz (Imaginary place)—Juvenile literature.   [1. Baum,
L. Frank (Lyman Frank), 1856–1919. Wizard of Oz.   2. American literature—
History and criticism.   3. Oz (Imaginary place)]   I. Glassman, Peter
II. Series.

PS3503.A923 W636   2000   99-87236
813'.4—dc21

Typography by Al Cetta
1 2 3 4 5 6 7 8 9 10
❖
First Edition

CONTENTS

Introduction by Peter Glassman vii

Art by Maurice Sendak vii

Art by Janell Cannon 3

Words and art by Tomie dePaola 5

Words and art by Jerry Pinkney 7

Words and art by Paul O. Zelinsky 8

Words and art by Uri Shulevitz 10

Words and art by Trina Schart Hyman 12

Words and art by William Joyce 14

Words and art by Richard Egielski 17

Words and art by Diane Goode 18

Words by Robin McKinley 19

Art by Leo and Diane Dillon 20

Words by Madeleine L'Engle 21

Words and art by Mark Teague 23

Words and art by Jules Feiffer 24

Words by Ann M. Martin 25

Words and art by Kinuko Y. Craft 27

Words and art by Kay Chorao 28

Words and art by Michael Foreman 31

Art by Mark Buehner 32

Words by Natalie Babbitt 33

Words and art by Peter Sís 34

Words and art by Bruce Degen 37

Art by Chris Van Allsburg 38

Words and art by Michael Hague 40

Words and art by Troy Howell 43

Words and art by Richard Jesse Watson 45

Words and art by Lloyd Alexander 46

Words and art by Eric Carle 48

About the authors and illustrators 49

INTRODUCTION

Just say the word and images filled with wonder and enchantment leap to mind. It is hard to imagine that the magical land of Oz is celebrating its one hundredth anniversary. On the one hand, Oz is so timeless, so enduring, that it seems as though it must have always been around, just like the classic fairy tales and the legends of King Arthur and the Arabian Nights. And yet the stories written by L. Frank Baum—with their female protagonists, fascination with technology, and reverence for the natural world— read so well today that it seems that they might have been written just recently.

L. Frank Baum did not set out to be a children's book author. He tried his hand at many different careers—actor, playwright, crockery salesman, journalist, store owner, axle-grease manufacturer—but none with much success. Then, at the age of forty, Frank discovered his true calling: the writing of books for children. In a copy of his first children's book, *Mother Goose in Prose*, Baum inscribed, "To please a child is a sweet and lovely thing that warms one's heart and brings its own reward." Surely Baum's Oz eventually warmed not only his own heart, but the hearts of *billions* of children and adults who have visited his magical fairyland in one form or another.

Over the past fifteen years, as we republished the Oz books, I came to discover that many of the children's book authors and artists whose work I most admired are also big fans of Oz. This book is an homage by these great talents to the enchanted land that inspired them and helped shape their imaginations. For it is Baum's incredible imagination, mixed with W. W. Denslow's and John R. Neill's fanciful illustrations, that started many of these wonderful talents down their own Yellow Brick Road. In these pages you will discover the special place Oz holds in the hearts of so many of today's finest authors and artists.

Whether it's six-year-old Kay Chorao, miserable and bored after breaking her arm, entranced by her big brother reading aloud to her from *The Wonderful Wizard of Oz*; or young Uri Shulevitz, fleeing to Russia from Nazi-occupied Poland and having the story fed to him like food by a friend; or Robin McKinley, discovering a girl who did not wait for someone to rescue her, but instead did the rescuing herself, Oz was a major influence on each child's life. For Lloyd Alexander and Paul O. Zelinsky, Oz provided inspiration in their own childhoods and then a

Art by Maurice Sendak

priceless opportunity to share a magical place with their children. For each and every one of the authors and artists included here, Oz has touched their hearts.

One way or another, Oz has touched all of our lives. Much as *Alice in Wonderland* became the children's book by which the British identify themselves and their culture, so too has Oz—and especially Dorothy, the Scarecrow, the Tin Woodman, and the Cowardly Lion—become a metaphor for aspects of the modern American experience. Almost from the very beginning, Oz has had a life beyond the books. In 1902 it became a smash hit stage musical. In the 1920s it was made as a silent film, with Oliver Hardy playing the Tin Man. And, of course, in 1939 Metro-Goldwyn-Mayer released the classic movie musical starring Judy Garland as Dorothy. Between its annual airings on television since the 1960s and more recently its availability on videocassette, the MGM film is one of the most viewed movies of all time.

Everywhere you look you can find elements of Oz. Be it television commercials, political cartoons, peanut butter jars, books on business philosophy, or even the offbeat comic strips of Gary Larson's *The Far Side*, Oz continues to pop up throughout American society.

Though Oz is quintessentially American, it has an appeal that is universal. For a young Peter Sís, trapped behind the Iron Curtain, and a young Michael Foreman, caught in the Nazi bombings of his home in England, Oz was an image of hope and courage. *The Wonderful Wizard of Oz* and its successors have been published in so many different languages that it would be difficult to find a language in which Oz has not appeared.

Special thanks must go to each and every one of the authors and artists who so generously donated their time and talent to create this book. It is not only a testament to their love of Oz, but also to their admiration of the great work being done by Reading Is Fundamental (RIF), which receives proceeds from the sale of this book. As the nation's oldest and most influential charity devoted to children's literacy, RIF has helped millions of children begin their own journeys down the Yellow Brick Road of reading.

So here's to Oz! Happy hundredth birthday. May Ozma's reign last many hundreds more.

—*Peter Glassman*

The HUNDREDth
ANNIVERSARY
CELEBRATION

I was one of many children of the late '30s that came to the magical land of Oz by way of the MGM movie. I had been taken to the movies from the time I was two years old. My mother, Flossie, loved the movies (my dad could take them or leave them), and since the movies began at noon and prices were cheaper before 4:00 P.M., Mom took me with her in the early afternoons. I knew proper "movie etiquette" and even had my favorite stars—Miss Mae West and little Shirley Temple.

Nineteen thirty-eight was a banner movie year for me. Walt Disney's *Snow White and the Seven Dwarfs* came to the silver screen, and for four-year-old Tomie, it was the *best* movie I had ever seen.

My mom, who kept in touch with what was going on in Hollywood through her monthly magazines, told me about the upcoming filming of L. Frank Baum's *Wonderful Wizard of Oz*. I didn't know anything about that story. She hadn't read it to me yet. But I certainly was interested, because the talk was that my fave, Shirley Temple, was going to be in it *and* that it would be in TECHNICOLOR!

Well, Shirley didn't play Dorothy. Another young star did—and Judy Garland joined my list of favorites. I knew all the words of "Somewhere Over the Rainbow," and *The Wizard of Oz* became the other *best* movie I had ever seen.

Of course, the books were eventually read to me, and I developed my own ideas about the whole Oz thing. It turned out that the Scarecrow, the Tin Woodman, and the Cowardly Lion were not as fascinating to me as Jack Pumpkinhead and the Wooden Sawhorse.

And why not TOMIE going down the Yellow Brick Road instead of Dorothy, or Judy, or even Shirley! Oh, Toto could come, but my bodyguard would be Jack Pumpkinhead on the Sawhorse.

But sorry, Mr. Baum—*ruby* slippers still thrill me more than the original silver ones!

Words and art by Tomie dePaola

The lion—his mane a crown on his head—appears fearless and majestic, ruling over all the creatures of the forest, large and small. Yet even the king of the jungle can see himself as a coward.

Where do these feelings of cowardice come from? He certainly exhibits bravery in his deeds on the way to visit Oz. If only he could see himself in the way his actions demonstrate, for the deeds of someone who is frightened but still responds are the most courageous of all.

The king of the jungle need only look inside himself. There he'll find a hero—one who acts with bravery in spite of fear.

Words and art
by Jerry Pinkney

Dorothy Gale's Kansas is in the middle of "Tornado Alley." The northern end of it, in Illinois, is where I grew up. Not an autumn passed without a twister or two threatening our neighborhood and frightening me down to my bones. That's one reason the movie of *The Wizard of Oz* meant so much to me: in its stormy opening, Dorothy's terror was my terror. And when I was reader enough to take on the Oz books, I read through them avidly, all the ones our library owned.

That was so long ago I don't recall most of what I read. But I do remember wondering what was in the Oz books that weren't in the library or in the bookstore.

Eventually I was to find out. I married and became a father, and the time came to read Oz out loud, one chapter a night at bedtime. Anna couldn't get enough of the books, and I couldn't have had a better time reading to her. There is something exhilarating about the work of a truly original imagination—L. Frank Baum's all but overflowed with marvels. Beyond the famous characters in *The Wonderful Wizard of Oz* there were so many others just as memorable: the mechanical Tik-Tok, whose thought, speech, and action all wound down and needed cranking up independently; the Thoroughly Educated Wogglebug, enlarged from bug size after being placed in a slide projector; poor Jack Pumpkinhead, who never knew when his head might start to rot—all brought out with such matter-of-fact, unimpeachable logic that they seem less like creations than discoveries.

Anna and I read through one Oz book after another, until one day she took off on her own and finished all of the Oz books that Baum wrote. Then she started with the first one and read them again. And again.

Four years later, little Rachel repeated Anna's Oz experience. And after a few books, I would have to skip a chapter between readings—she had read ahead during the day. Then I'd have to skip several chapters, and more and more. It finally became too confusing to me, and Rachel took over the reading of Oz on her own. She and Anna haven't needed to wonder about what was in the later books; we have them on the shelf. How wonderful that Oz is still in print!

Words and art by Paul O. Zelinsky

When the Nazis invaded Poland, my parents and I fled to Russia. In the last year of the war I was ten years old and living in Central Asia. Food was scarce. I compensated for the lack of food by reading stories. I had no books, but I had a friend who did. After school I would visit him.

He lived in a house with a courtyard, surrounded by high walls of clay. A huge tree grew in the middle, shading most of the courtyard. There was also a large, fierce dog on a chain. The first time I visited my friend, the dog came running menacingly at me, barking and baring his sharp teeth. It was rather intimidating. I walked cautiously, my back hugging the wall, making sure I was out of his reach.

Although I was scared of the dog, I was eager to return for another chapter of *The Wonderful Wizard of Oz*, and to forget hunger and war. My friend read me in Russian a chapter a week. I couldn't wait for the next week and the next chapter. And so weeks passed. The war ended, and it was time for us to leave Central Asia. But in spite of the promise of food, I was reluctant to return to Eastern Europe without knowing if Dorothy was able to return to Kansas. . . .

Words and art by Uri Shulevitz

Words and art by Trina Schart Hyman

The history of Mr. Baum's Oz books is packed with improbable good luck stories, but this one is hands down the spookiest.

During the filming of the 1939 movie version of *The Wizard of Oz*, Frank Morgan, who played the part of the Wizard, was dissatisfied with the coat the costume department supplied him. Mr. Morgan went to a secondhand clothing store in downtown Hollywood and found a turn-of-the-century coat that fit the character of the Wizard perfectly.

Several days later, during a break in filming, he happened to notice a tag sewn onto the inside pocket. His jaw dropped. It read "L. F. Baum." He had found Frank Baum's actual coat!

Baum, it turned out, had lived for some years in Hollywood, not far from that same secondhand store.

Pay no attention to that man behind the curtain? I don't know about that.

Words and art by William Joyce

There were few books in our home when I was growing up, and even fewer children's books. So my first encounter with *The Wonderful Wizard of Oz* was seeing the movie on our small black-and-white television. I remember loving the story, but I was horrified by the witch's ghastly grinning flying monkeys. To me they were scarier than Frankenstein, Dracula, or the Wolf Man. Well, maybe not as scary as the Wolf Man. . . .

But that night, as I lay in my bed and heard the breeze stir the curtains, I was sure that a flying monkey was hovering over me, ready to pounce. My only defense to such phantoms—whether flying monkeys, bogeymen in the closet, or zombies under my bed—was to lie absolutely still. The slightest movement would be the end of me. Eventually I fell asleep, and in the morning, the flying monkey was gone.

Words and art by Richard Egielski

I never thought a little girl like you would ever be able to melt me and end my wicked deeds. Look out—here I go!"

I love this witch. She is afraid of the dark and she won't touch water. Was *she* ever in for a surprise! But who is more surprised in this scene, Dorothy or the Wicked Witch of the West? They both realize at the same instant that Dorothy possesses a power she had heretofore been unaware of. To me, it is absolutely wonderful! And, to top it all, good triumphs over evil. What could be more satisfying?

Words and art by Diane Goode

The thing about Oz, for me, was Dorothy. When I was a child I was looking for Girls Who Did Things. Most of the books I read seemed to be about boys having adventures and girls staying at home and being good, i.e. boring, and not having adventures—if girls existed at all, which frequently they did not. I grew very accustomed to identifying with boy heroes, but I didn't like it much.

I was a military brat and an only child, and grew up moving on every year or two. Very early I decided that the real world was far too unstable to pay more than idle attention to—very nice, I'm sure, but I'm just passing through. A book, though, was the same book as it was the last time you opened its pages, in Hawaii or Rhode Island or Germany, last year or next year. I particularly liked long books or series where you could really get inside and move around and learn about the place and the people, and figure out where you might fit in if you lived there. For more than a year or two.

I was hooked from the first time I read *The Wizard of Oz*. When Dorothy rushes up and slaps the Lion on the nose to protect Toto and the Scarecrow and the Tin Man, it was better than St. George slaying the dragon (with the stupid princess tied to a tree) and Perseus stabbing the sea monster (with another stupid princess chained to a rock) and Sir Lancelot tilting at everything that moved (with Guinevere bound to a stake), all wrapped up in one.

And Oz was full of wonders, people and creatures and magic, especially for a girl who was tired of boys' adventures. In my dreams I was just like Dorothy, brave and honest and clever and steadfast and indefatigable. Although perhaps my favorite story of all, from *Ozma of Oz*, isn't about Dorothy, but her friend Billina, the yellow hen, who saves not only the queen of Ev and all her children from the wicked and powerful Nome King, but Ozma of Oz and her army—and Dorothy—too. If a *hen* could be a hero, then there was hope even for a girl who wasn't always brave and honest and clever and steadfast and indefatigable.

I was rolling now.

Words by Robin McKinley

Whan I hear the word "Oz," I see myself in a small back bedroom in a New York apartment with the window looking out on a courtyard and the windows of other apartment buildings. Far beyond this bleak view lay the more real one of the world of Oz. Like many native Manhattanites, I knew very little about the rest of the country, and the idea of a bleak landscape where a tornado could sweep a house off its foundations was as alien to me as the landscape of the moon.

But perhaps the most important thing I learned was that I, like the Cowardly Lion, could learn to be brave; like the Tin Woodman, I could get a real heart; and like the Scarecrow, maybe one day I would have a brain and the teachers would stop thinking me the stupid one.

I am glad that in the book what Dorothy did was real and true and not just a dream, because I believed then, and I still do, that what I do in my world of imagination is far more real and far more true than any dream. L. Frank Baum knew that most reluctantly accepted truth: that story is indeed our vehicle of truth, and far more real than the limited world of provable fact.

Words by Madeleine L'Engle

< Art by Leo and Diane Dillon

I grew up in southern California, far from Oz—or even Kansas, for that matter. But it made no difference. Magical places have their own logic. There was always a chance I might find my way there. Trudging toward school on Monday morning I had my eyes peeled.

Words and art by Mark Teague

So these little guys - they call themselves "Munchkins" - they agreed with me that it wasn't actually my fault the witch was dead, the house did it. Even if it is my house, how can I be guilty for what a house does? I mean, come on! But they said, it looked bad and maybe I better get away and they pointed out this yellow-brick road, OK?...

Go on, Dorothy...

Words and art by Jules Feiffer

I am sitting at my desk with the four Wizard of Oz books I was given as a child: *The Land of Oz*, *Ozma of Oz*, *The Road to Oz*, and *Tik-Tok of Oz*. I am recalling how my love affair with the Wizard of Oz began. It began with the books. The movie undoubtedly enhanced it, but it began with these four books. They are hardcovers. *Tik-Tok* is still encased in its jacket; it was priced at $3.50. I didn't own the very first book about Oz, variously called *The Wizard in Oz*, *Dorothy and the Wizard in Oz*, *The Wonderful Wizard of Oz*, and of course *The Wizard of Oz*, but I had borrowed it from our public library, had read it and loved it, and then had read a great many of the other books about Oz. The flyleaf of *Tik-Tok* listed thirty-eight titles. I dutifully checked off the ones I read.

I was as fascinated by the books themselves as I was by the stories about Oz. I remember sprawling in my bedroom in the summertime poring through the books. Not only were they tantalizingly illustrated by John R. Neill, including fanciful decorations on the copyright pages, dedication pages, and title pages, but a glance at the tables of contents yielded such wondrous names as General Jinjur, Dr. Nikidik, Billina, Langwidere, Ruggedo, the Scoodler, the Shaggy Man, and the Long-Eared Hearer. And then there were the notes to the reader written by L. Frank Baum himself. One told of Baum's promise to a little girl that he would write another Oz story (after the publication of *The Wonderful Wizard of Oz*) when he had received a thousand letters from children imploring him to do so. In another note, dated 1909, Baum claimed to be astonished by "some very remarkable news from The Land of Oz," which was to be the makings of another book. As if the notes weren't interesting enough, there were Baum's dedications—for instance, "To Louis F. Gottschalk, whose sweet and dainty melodies breathe the true spirit of fairyland." My personal favorite was the one in *Ozma of Oz*: "To all the boys and girls who read my stories—and especially to the Dorothys—this book is lovingly dedicated." I couldn't get over it. The book was dedicated to *me*.

It is now more than thirty-five years since I was introduced to the Wizard of Oz and since my love affair began. I have read and reread the books. I have sewn Dorothy costumes for young aspiring Dorothys. I frequently give the books as gifts. When I do, I try to find older editions, similar to the ones I read, so that the decorations and dedications and notes as well as the stories can be enjoyed by another generation of readers. My nephew isn't quite old enough to listen to the Wizard of Oz stories yet, but he will be soon. I'm waiting for him to fall in love too.

Words by Ann M. Martin

The Oz stories have always attracted me, from my earliest years. The fantastic never-never land Baum created was a place I loved to dream and fantasize about. Ozma was one of my favorite characters because of her thoughtful wisdom, grace, and beauty. I would have given anything to be able to meet her and visit the wonderful Emerald City. Now, finally, I have put on illustration board the image of her that I have carried around in my mind all of these years. It's as close as I can come to a real visit.

Words and art
by Kinuko Y. Craft

Many children's book writers and illustrators describe their early love for reading. They describe loving the look, feel, and even the smell of books. I did not. I disliked sitting still. What I loved was running, climbing, jumping, exploring, and almost anything else active.

But the summer I was six, I fell off a horse and broke my arm. It was June, with the hot Indiana summer stretching out endlessly, and my right arm was encased in plaster. I could not swim, ride my bike, climb the jungle gym, or even dash through the sprinkler. I was unbearably miserable, and bad-tempered.

Fortunately, my brother, Ron, then Ronny, loved books passionately and offered to read aloud to me. The book he started with was *The Wonderful Wizard of Oz*. I can imagine I squirmed and complained that there would be too many words, not enough pictures, when we started. But it was not long before I was entranced.

What I discovered was that the events unrolled so quickly, so clearly, that I could see the action and characters in my head, even with few illustrations.

I was fascinated by Dorothy.

"How old *is* she?" I asked my brother. What I really meant was, She must be much, much older than I am. She never whines or acts scared, and there she is, marching along stoutly in those silver shoes *with total strangers*, miles from home, with scary things popping up over and over.

"A little older than you," my brother said.

I stared at the illustration of the little girl with odd, lumpy braids.

"A lot older," I said, but I didn't believe that. Dorothy looked like Lucinda, a little girl with fat, glossy braids, which I coveted, in my class at school.

In any case, I knew that a girl who could handle witches and flying monkeys would never throw tantrums over a broken arm. I wanted to *be* Dorothy.

So I settled in next to my beloved brother and let the vivid words of Frank Baum help me forget the hateful plaster cast, weighing heavily in my lap. I was beginning to love books.

Words and art by Kay Chorao

oward the end of the Second World War, the *Wizard of Oz* movie came to our local cinema on the east coast of England. Our town was regularly bombed, and one of the cinemas had been blown up a few months earlier. Because of this my mother didn't allow me to go to the movies.

However, some of my friends did see the film and were inspired. The girls, who were always putting on shows, gave an impromptu concert and sang "Follow the Yellow Brick Road" and, of course, "Over the Rainbow."

I didn't see the film, nor read any of the Oz books, until I had children of my own, but the memory of those girls—Pat, Brenda, Rosemary, and April—singing in the rubble of war has stayed with me as an image of hope, of another world, and of Oz.

Words and art by Michael Foreman

I read my first Oz book, *The Wonderful Wizard of Oz*, when I was about eight years old, and liked it so much that I went on to read every single one of the others. They were all good, but my favorite was *The Emerald City of Oz*, which was already nearly thirty years old by the time I got around to it. What a wonderful man L. Frank Baum must have been! I don't know a thing about him or about his life, but it doesn't matter. The books tell what's important: that he knew how to tell a story and he knew how to make up entirely new creatures and entirely new kinds of magic.

When I was in grammar school, I loved to draw pictures of people and animals—I still do—so when I came to the part in *The Emerald City of Oz* that tells about Miss Cuttenclip, I fell in love and read her chapter again and again. Miss Cuttenclip has made a whole town out of magic paper, a town full of paper people and paper animals that are alive and can move about and talk—or bark and moo—even though they are only the size of regular paper dolls. This is just about the best magic I ever heard of.

In the same book there is a town called Fuddlecumjig where everybody is made like jigsaw puzzles. When they are surprised by something, they scatter themselves and then have to lie around in little pieces until someone comes along and puts them back together. The Lord High Chigglewitz, who is a sort of mayor, has a piece missing from his knee, so he walks with a limp. Perfectly reasonable. I loved jigsaw puzzles—I still do—so of course I loved Fuddlecumjig.

The "bad guy" in *The Emerald City of Oz* is the Nome King. He has a terrible temper and when he gets angry at someone, which happens very often, he calls in his guards and has them drag that someone out and throw him away. I liked the idea of throwing someone away. I still do. And I also liked the even more final punishment—a machine that slices your enemy into thin slices, after which he can be fed to the seven-headed dogs. Both punishments seemed neat and tidy to me. And reasonable.

I don't think there has been anyone so good at thinking up new creatures and new magic. The Tin Woodman, the Scarecrow, and the Cowardly Lion are only the first of many. And they are all reasonable. Magic and fantasy in stories are no good unless they are also reasonable. L. Frank Baum understood this better than anyone.

I just read *The Emerald City of Oz* again recently after almost fifty years because I remembered how fine and how reasonable I thought it was when I was in grammar school, and I wanted to see if I still thought so. Absolutely. I still do.

Words by Natalie Babbitt

< Art by Mark Buehner

OZ

PRAHA

I knew pictures from Oz ever since I was a little boy. Only I did not know what they were.

My grandfather kept them in the glass case with all the other children's books he had purchased for my mother and her brother in America. He had brought his family there from his home in Moravia in the 1930s while he worked on the design of the railways in Cleveland, Boston, and Chicago.

He brought his family back to Moravia, as he had promised, just before the start of World War II, and I was born there.

Grandfather Charles was a serious man and believed the books to be serious objects of education—to be kept clean and protected from dirty little hands (some of the books not locked in the glass case proved him right!). He would sometimes flip through the children's books, which looked and smelled so different, and that's how I remember the pictures of Oz.

Sadly, before I could truly understand, comprehend, or even just read, my grandfather departed from my life and I never saw the glass case again. Everything in my life changed. I saw no more traces of Oz, just red flags and red stars everywhere—the Iron Curtain was all around.

It took many years until, at the ripe age of twenty-five, I was lucky enough to be spending my first Christmas abroad. I was in England and they were showing on television—as they do every year—*The Wizard of Oz*. Not only did I fall in love with the film, but the moving images brought back the childhood memories of the pictures from my grandfather's book.

I had to return behind the Iron Curtain before finally leaving for good in 1982. Oz helped me to survive each of those days. Whenever the restrictions of the communist system became too oppressive, I would imagine I was the Scarecrow, Tin Woodman, or Cowardly Lion, depending upon the situation. And as soon as I had defeated the Wicked Witch, all these beloved characters would lead me to L. Frank Baum, the Sawhorse, Tik-Tok, the Gump, and Jack Pumpkinhead.

Now that I live in America, I explore Oz with my own two children—my seven-year-old daughter, who loves Dorothy, and my five-year-old son, who likes to be scared by the Wicked Witch.

Only now, ten years after the fall of communism, did I find out—by reading the recently published list of the "forbidden books" under the communists—why I was not able to see the translated books during my childhood. *The Wizard of Oz* was one of the many wonderful books stamped "ideologically incorrect" and therefore forbidden. Some others: *Alice in Wonderland*, *The Catcher in the Rye*, and *The Little Prince*.

Words and art by Peter Sís

Even when I was very young, I loved to watch scary movies. But at night, as I lay in bed in my very dark and quiet bedroom in Brooklyn, I was sure that the latest monster or Martian was lurking in the shadows. One false move, one slip of the blanket exposing my neck, and Dracula would leap for my jugular.

While watching the movie *The Wizard of Oz* I found the flying monkeys swooping down on the heroes graceful, scary, and unforgettable. For years after, I was sure that they would come into the dark bedroom and lift me, bed and all, and carry me away. Not through the window, which was too small, but exploding through the roof. Never mind that old Mrs. Mersant lived upstairs, and that bed, boy, and beasts would have to crash through her floor and ceiling on our way to the castle of the Wicked Witch of the West. Those flying monkeys couldn't be stopped.

Words and art by Bruce Degen

Art by Chris Van Allsburg

I love beginnings. My favorite part of any book is when the heroes begin their quest. The illustration I chose to do for the Oz book is that very moment when Dorothy has chosen to take destiny in her hands and walk down the Yellow Brick Road.

A stranger in a strange land, our Dorothy sets out bravely on her quest to reach the Emerald City. The light mark upon her forehead is the kiss from the Good Witch of the North. It is her hall pass through the bizarre and wonderful world of Oz.

*Words and art
by Michael Hague*

DOROTHY AND THE SILVER SHOES

Twinkle, twinkle, myriad stars
Upon two silver shoes;
I wish I may in wondrous flight
Away to where I choose.
A tap together of the heels,
A yearning of the soul,
And through a moment's passageway
Across the heavens stroll.
No place go I—exotic, rare,
Exceeding great or fine—
No place, but to a simple state,
Modest by design.
No other comforts capture me,
No other people share
The plain familiarity,
The unassuming care.
The evening star above my bed,
Beneath my feet the loam
That holds the seed that grows the life:
The place I call my home.

Words and art by Troy Howell

round and around the chicken coop the Wicked Witch of the East is chasing me. The next thing I know, my dad varooms up in our yellow 1949 GMC Carry-All truck, rescues me, then drives us deep into the heart of a mountain and chases the demons and goblins away. . . .

Pop was not the kind of wizard who turned lead into gold. Rather he turned our gold into gadgets and gallimaufry inventions: from gages to Geiger counters, from gyroscopes to gene machines.

When a preoccupied wizard baby-sits a munchkin, wahoo for the munchkin! To keep me entertained as a lad, I was given steel rods and told to go play with the five-horsepower grinder, with which I would shower my little feet with glorious sparks. When bored of that, other playthings appeared: strobe lights, black lights, liquid mercury (which he did say was poison), dry ice, magnets, soldering irons, Bunsen burners, and generally a good part of the periodic table. My favorite display was tossing chunks of metallic Na into H_2O until *fheeezzle-sput-sput-sputter-KAPOW!!! KABOOSH!!!!*

Another great and terrible toy that had a calming effect on me was a 50,000-volt vacuum-leak tester. ("It's pretty safe; low amps," said the wiz.) A virtual ray gun. I could *d-d-d-zzzapp!* this, *d-d-d-zzzapp!* that. Ahhh . . . the smell of ozone. A boy in bliss.

On long car trips the wize one cooked us meals by placing canned foods around the engine block. At home he cooked turkeys using his solar oven. Never mind burning up the patio when he forgot to cover the great and terrible mirrors one hot afternoon.

When Dad reached the land of octogenaria some of his electrons sought asylum elsewhere. One day at the radial-arm saw he sawed off three fingers. Ever the philosopher, he kept them in an olive jar with formaldehyde. "Well, one day he went up in his balloon and couldn't come down again. And I assume he went way up above the clouds and awoke to find the balloon floating over a strange and beautiful country."

Words and art by Richard Jesse Watson

I began my journey through Oz by lucky accident. Usually for my birthday I received socks, handkerchiefs, or other equally sensible and boring gifts. But that year—I must have been about nine or ten—one of my aunts gave me *The Wonderful Wizard of Oz*. Why? Out of last-minute desperation? The inspired suggestion of a bookseller? A sudden shortage of handkerchiefs? I have no idea. No matter, I plunged into that marvelous world, reveled in it, and demanded more.

During the following months, I whined, pleaded, begged, and sniveled so efficiently that several more Oz books were cautiously doled out to me. My family were all enthusiastic nonreaders, convinced that books could overheat the imagination and spoil a young mind for the practical realities of life. Oz was eventually discontinued. I never did read all the series. But—too late. The damage was done. I had discovered a world of joyous wonders. I knew the stories by heart and could rejoin my dear friends by simply thinking about them: not only the Scarecrow, Tin Woodman, Cowardly Lion, and Dorothy, but also Jack Pumpkinhead, the Sawhorse, Tik-Tok—and the Gump, especially fascinating because it looked very much like the sofa in our living room. Indeed, I used to climb onto that sofa and make believe it was carrying me through the air. As it did. At least in my imagination.

In the course of time, I left Oz and did not return for some dozen years. By then, I had grown up, survived World War II, lived in France, and had married there. When I, my Parisian wife, Janine, and her beautiful little daughter, Mado, finally sailed back to Drexel Hill, Pennsylvania, we took up living quarters in my parents' attic. While I struggled to become a writer, Janine and Mado struggled even harder to learn English. To help them, I dug out some of my childhood books, including, of course, my Oz collection. Its magic captivated them as it had captivated me long before, far beyond the practical purpose of learning a new language. I delighted in Oz all over again. I took my daughter flying on the Gump (we still had the same old sofa in the living room). Our favorite cry of warning or alarm was "Watch out for the Wheelers!"

I realize I have been telling about events of more than fifty years ago. But, even as I write this, Oz comes back to me as fresh and bright as it ever was. My old Oz books are gone; some handed down to my grandchildren; some fallen to shreds by constant rereadings; some mysteriously vanished into the cavernous depths of the attic, lost under the eaves. No, not lost. They haven't vanished at all. They're happily and permanently in my heart. Which is exactly where they belong.

Words and art by Lloyd Alexander

GREETINGS FROM
THE VERY HUNGRY CATERPILLAR
TO ALL HIS FRIENDS OF
THE WONDERFUL
WIZARD OF OZ ——
ON THEIR
100TH BIRTHDAY

ERIC CARLE

ABOUT THE AUTHORS AND ILLUSTRATORS

< Words and art by Eric Carle

All the wonderful artists and authors whose creative efforts make up *Oz: The Hundredth Anniversary Celebration* generously contributed their work to this project. Among them, they have won hundreds of awards for their many beloved books.

LLOYD ALEXANDER's "Chronicles of Prydain" consists of five fantasy novels: *The High King* (1968), winner of the Newbery Medal; *Taran Wanderer* (1967); *The Castle of Llyr* (1966); *The Black Cauldron* (1965), a Newbery Honor Book; and *The Book of Three* (1964). Among his many other novels and picture books for young readers are *The Arkadians* (1995) and *The Fortune-tellers* (1992).

NATALIE BABBITT's novel *Knee-Knock Rise* (1970) was named a Newbery Honor Book. Her novel *Tuck Everlasting* (1975), about the discovery of a fountain of youth by a ten-year-old girl, has been acclaimed as a modern classic. She is also the author of *The Search for Delicious* (1969) and *The Devil's Storybook* (1974), as well as the author-illustrator of the picture book *Nellie: A Cat on Her Own* (1989).

MARK BUEHNER's books include *My Monster Mama Loves Me So* (1999), by Laura Leuck; *It's a Spoon, Not a Shovel* (1995), by Caralyn Buehner; and *The Adventures of Taxi Dog* (1990), by Debra and Sal Barracca.

JANELL CANNON has written and illustrated many books, among them *Stellaluna* (1993), an American Booksellers Association ABBY winner; *Trupp: A Fuzzhead Tale* (1995); *Verdi* (1997); and *Crickwing* (2000).

ERIC CARLE is known especially for his enormously popular "Very" stories, including *The Very Hungry Caterpillar* (1979). His other books include *Does a Kangaroo Have a Mother, Too?* (2000); *The Grouchy Ladybug* (1977); *From Head to Toe* (1997); *Papa, Please Get the Moon for Me* (1986); *Do You Want to Be My Friend?* (1971); *The Mixed-Up Chameleon* (1984); and *The Secret Birthday Message* (1972); and *Brown Bear, Brown Bear, What Do You See?* (1967) by Bill Martin, Jr.

KAY CHORAO's books for young readers include *The Baby's Lap Book* (1977) and *The Baby's Story Book* (1985); *The Good-Bye Book* (1988), by Judith Viorst; and *The Book of Giving: Poems of Thanks, Praise, and Celebration* (1995).

KINUKO Y. CRAFT has illustrated a number of children's books, including *The Twelve Dancing Princesses* (1989) and *Pegasus* (1998), both by Marianna Mayer; and *King Midas and the Golden Touch* (1999) and *Cupid and Psyche* (1996), both by Charlotte Craft.

BRUCE DEGEN's picture books include *Jamberry* (1983) and *Sailaway Home* (1996). He has collaborated with Joanna Cole on books in the Magic School Bus series, and he is the illustrator of the Jesse Bear books of Nancy White Carlstrom, including *Better Not Get Wet, Jesse Bear* (1988) and *Jesse Bear, What Will You Wear?* (1986).

TOMIE dePAOLA is the illustrator of over 200 books for children. His *Strega Nona* (1975) was named a Caldecott Honor Book, and *26 Fairmount Avenue* (1999) was named a Newbery Honor Book. Among his other books are *Nana Upstairs & Nana Downstairs* (1973/new edition 1998), *The Clown of God* (1978), and *Tomie dePaola's Mother Goose* (1985). A retrospective look at his work, *Tomie dePaola, His Art & His Stories*, by Barbara Elleman, was published in 1999.

DIANE and LEO DILLON have collaborated on the illustrations for two Caldecott Medal–winning books: *Ashanti to Zulu: African Traditions* (1976), by Margaret Musgrove, and *Why Mosquitoes Buzz in People's Ears* (1975), retold by Verna Aardema. Together they illustrated

Wind Child (1999), by Shirley R. Murphy; *To Everything There Is a Season* (1998); and *Aïda* (1990), retold by Leontyne Price.

RICHARD EGIELSKI illustrated the Caldecott Medal winner *Hey, Al* (1986), by Arthur Yorinks. He is the illustrator of the Tub People series, by Pam Conrad, including *The Tub People* (1989) and *The Tub People's Christmas* (1999). He has written as well as illustrated such picture books as *Buz* (1995), *Jazper* (1998), and *The Gingerbread Boy* (1997).

JULES FEIFFER is a children's book author and illustrator, syndicated cartoonist, playwright, and screenwriter. He illustrated *The Phantom Tollbooth* (1961), by Norton Juster, and wrote and illustrated the picture books *Bark, George* (1999); *I Lost My Bear* (1998); and *Meanwhile . . .* (1997). He is also the creator of *The Man in the Ceiling* (1993) and *A Barrel of Laughs, A Vale of Tears* (1995).

MICHAEL FOREMAN is the illustrator of the Kate Greenaway Medal winners *Sleeping Beauty and Other Favourite Fairy Tales* (1982), by Angela Carter, and *War Boy: A Country Childhood* (1989). His other books include *Michael Foreman's Mother Goose* (1991) and *War Game* (1994). He has also illustrated versions of the classic tales *Peter Pan and Wendy* (1988), by J. M. Barrie; *A Christmas Carol* (1983), by Charles Dickens; and *The Arabian Nights* (1995), by Brian Alderson.

DIANE GOODE illustrated the Caldecott Honor Book *When I Was Young in the Mountains* (1982), by Cynthia Rylant. Her other books include *The Dinosaur's New Clothes* (1999); *A Child's Garden of Verses* (1998), by Robert Louis Stevenson; *Diane Goode's Book of Giants and Little People* (1997); and *Mama's Perfect Present* (1996).

MICHAEL HAGUE has illustrated several books by William Bennett, including *The Children's Book of Virtues* (1995). He has collaborated with his wife, Kathleen Hague, on picture books such as *Alphabears* (1984) and *Numbears* (1986). He has also illustrated classics such as Hugh Lofting's *The Story of Doctor Dolittle* (1997), J. M. Barrie's *Peter Pan* (1987), and J. R. R. Tolkien's *The Hobbit* (1984), and collections such as *The Book of Dragons* (1995) and *Michael Hague's Family Christmas Treasury* (1995).

TROY HOWELL has illustrated several Mary Pope Osborne collections, including *Favorite Greek Myths* (1989), *Favorite Norse Myths* (1996), and *Mermaid Tales from Around the World* (1993). He has also illustrated *Redwall* (1997), by Brian Jacques.

TRINA SCHART HYMAN is the illustrator of the Caldecott Medal winner *Saint George and the Dragon* (1984), retold by Margaret Hodges. Her books *A Child's Calendar* (1999), by John Updike, *Hershel and the Hanukkah Goblins* (1989), by Eric Kimmel, and *Little Red Riding Hood* (1983) were named Caldecott Honor books. She has illustrated many classics of children's literature, including Howard Pyle's *King Stork* (1973) and *Bearskin* (1997).

WILLIAM JOYCE is an author and illustrator of noted children's books, a *New Yorker* cover artist, and a writer-producer of motion pictures. His award-winning books include *Rolie Polie Olie* (1999), *The Leaf Men* (1996), *Santa Calls* (1993), *Bently & egg* (1992), *Dinosaur Bob* (1989), and *George Shrinks* (1985). He also created the Emmy Award–winning animated TV series *Rolie Polie Olie* for the Disney Channel.

MADELEINE L'ENGLE is the author of the Newbery Medal winner *A Wrinkle in Time* (1962) and its companions, including *A Swiftly Tilting Planet* (1978), as well as *A Ring of Endless Light* (1980), a Newbery Honor Book, and many other books for young readers. In addition, she has written adult fiction, poetry, prayers and meditations, and nonfiction.

ANN M. MARTIN is the author of the Baby-sitters Club series, as well as a number of other titles for young readers, including *Leo the Magnificat* (1996), *Rachel Parker, Kindergarten Show-off* (1992), and *Ten Kids, No Pets* (1988).

ROBIN McKINLEY is the author of *The Hero and the Crown* (1985), which received the Newbery Medal, and *The Blue Sword* (1982), named a Newbery Honor Book. Her many other books include *Beauty* (1978), *The Outlaws of Sherwood* (1988), *Rose Daughter* (1997), and *Spindle's End* (2000).

JERRY PINKNEY has illustrated four Caldecott Honor books: *The Ugly Duckling* (1999) by Hans Christian Andersen; *John Henry* (1994), by Julius Lester; *Mirandy and Brother Wind* (1988), by Patricia C. McKissack; and *The Talking Eggs* (1989), by Robert D. San Souci. He retold and illustrated Rudyard Kipling's *Rikki-Tikki-Tavi* (1997), and his other books include *Sam and the Tigers* (1996), by Julius Lester, and *Back Home* (1992), by Gloria Jean Pinkney.

MAURICE SENDAK's classic picture book *Where the Wild Things Are* (1963) received the Caldecott Medal in 1964. Among the seven books he illustrated that are Caldecott Honor books are *Outside Over There* (1981); *In the Night Kitchen* (1970); and *Mr. Rabbit and the Lovely Present* (1962), by Charlotte Zolotow. In 1970, Maurice Sendak received the international Hans Christian Andersen Medal for illustration, and he remains the only American ever awarded this honor. He also received a 1996 National Medal of Arts in recognition of his contribution to the arts in America.

URI SHULEVITZ illustrated the Caldecott Medal winner *The Fool of the World and the Flying Ship* (1968), retold by Arthur Ransome. His books *Snow* (1998) and *The Treasure* (1978) were named Caldecott Honor books. Among his many other books are *Dawn* (1974), *The Secret Room* (1993), *Hosni the Dreamer* (1997), and *The Golden Goose* (1995).

PETER SÍS is the author-illustrator of two Caldecott Honor books: *Tibet: Through the Red Box* (1998) and *Starry Messenger* (1996). His other books include *Ship Ahoy!* (1999) and *Fire Truck* (1998), as well as several books by Jack Prelutsky, including *The Dragons Are Singing Tonight* (1993) and *The Gargoyle on the Roof* (1999).

MARK TEAGUE's books for young readers include *One Halloween Night* (1999), *The Lost and Found* (1998), *How I Spent My Summer Vacation* (1995), *Pigsty* (1994), and the Poppleton books, by Cynthia Rylant.

CHRIS VAN ALLSBURG is the creator of two Caldecott Medal–winning books: *The Polar Express* (1985) and *Jumanji* (1981). His book *The Garden of Abdul Gasazi* (1979) was named a Caldecott Honor Book. His other books include *Bad Day at Riverbend* (1995); *A City in Winter* (1996), by Mark Helprin; *The Sweetest Fig* (1993); *The Widow's Broom* (1992); and many more.

RICHARD JESSE WATSON has illustrated *One Wintry Night* (1994), by Ruth Bell Graham; *Tom Thumb* (1989), which won the Golden Kite Award; *The High Rise Glorious Skittle Skat Roarious Sky Pie Angel Food Cake* (1990), by Nancy Willard; and several other books.

PAUL O. ZELINSKY received the Caldecott Medal for his book *Rapunzel* (1997). Three books that he illustrated have been named Caldecott Honor books: *Swamp Angel* (1994), by Anne Isaacs; *Hansel and Gretel* (1984), retold by Rika Lesser; and *Rumpelstiltskin* (1986). He has illustrated several titles by Beverly Cleary, including the Newbery Medal–winning *Dear Mr. Henshaw* (1983). His other books include *The Wheels on the Bus* (1990) and two classic E. Nesbit stories, *The Enchanted Castle* (1992) and *Five Children and It* (1999).

THE WONDERFUL WIZARD OF OZ
by L. Frank Baum
with 24 full-color plates
and over 130 two-color illustrations
by W. W. Denslow

DOROTHY AND THE WIZARD IN OZ
by L. Frank Baum
with 16 full-color plates
and 50 black-and-white illustrations
by John R. Neill

THE MARVELOUS LAND OF OZ
by L. Frank Baum
with 16 full-color plates
and over 125 black-and-white illustrations
by John R. Neill

THE ROAD TO OZ
by L. Frank Baum
with 126 black-and-white illustrations
on multicolored paper
by John R. Neill

OZMA OF OZ
by L. Frank Baum
with 42 full-color and
21 two-color illustrations
by John R. Neill

THE EMERALD CITY OF OZ
by L. Frank Baum
with 16 full-color plates
and 90 black-and-white illustrations
by John R. Neill

THE PATCHWORK GIRL OF OZ
by L. Frank Baum
with 51 full-color and
80 black-and-white illustrations
by John R. Neill

RINKITINK IN OZ
by L. Frank Baum
with 12 full-color plates
and 97 black-and-white illustrations
by John R. Neill

TIK-TOK OF OZ
by L. Frank Baum
with 12 full-color plates
and 78 black-and-white illustrations
by John R. Neill

THE LOST PRINCESS OF OZ
by L. Frank Baum
with 12 full-color plates
and 98 black-and-white illustrations
by John R. Neill

THE SCARECROW OF OZ
by L. Frank Baum
with 12 full-color plates
and 104 black-and-white illustrations
by John R. Neill

THE TIN WOODMAN OF OZ
by L. Frank Baum
with 12 full-color plates
and 92 black-and-white illustrations
by John R. Neill

THE MAGIC OF OZ
by L. Frank Baum
with 12 full-color plates
and 104 black-and-white illustrations
by John R. Neill

LITTLE WIZARD STORIES OF OZ
by L. Frank Baum
with 45 full-color illustrations
by John R. Neill

GLINDA OF OZ
by L. Frank Baum
with 12 full-color plates
and 91 black-and-white illustrations
by John R. Neill

DOROTHY OF OZ
by Roger S. Baum
with full-color frontispiece
and 50 black-and-white illustrations
by Elizabeth Miles

If you enjoy the Oz books and want to know more about Oz, you may be interested in
The Royal Club of Oz. Devoted to America's favorite fairyland, it is a club for everyone who loves
the Oz books. For free information, please send a first-class stamp to:

The Royal Club of Oz
P.O. Box 714
New York, New York 10011
or call toll free: (800) 207-6968